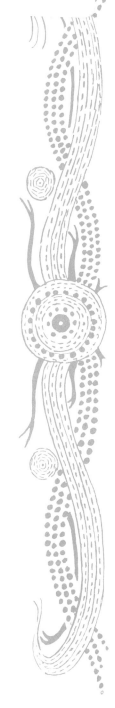

The Dream

Rae Harris
with
Beryl Harp

Magabala Books

First published 1991
Magabala Books Aboriginal Corporation,
PO Box 668, Broome, Western Australia 6725

Magabala Books receives financial assistance from the Government of Western Australia,
through the Department for the Arts, the Aboriginal and Torres Strait Islander Commission
and the Australia Council, the Federal Government's arts funding and advisory body.
Magabala Books gratefully acknowledges the support of Apple Computer Australia
in the provision of Apple Macintosh equipment.

Designer Carol Tang Wei
Editor Peter Bibby
Production Coordinator Merrilee Lands
Reproduction Victor France Photographics
Nyungar language consultants Glenys Collard and Dr Alan Dench
Printed by Kyodo Printing Co, Singapore
Typeset in 14pt Palatino

National Library of Australia
Cataloguing-in-Publication Data

Harris, Rae, 1905 -
The dream.

ISBN 0 9588101 6 8.

I. Harp, Beryl. II. Title.

A823.3

To Diney, who inspired this book

Characters in the Dream

Wardangmaat	....	Crow People; *wardang* is 'crow', the *maat* (literally 'leg') ending means 'people in the crow line'
Mandjang	....	Elders (women)
Burang	....	Elders (men)
Yok Dwongkabula	....	Wise Woman; it means 'much understanding ears'
Mamang	....	Great Spirit, Father (of all things)
Nurunderi	....	Ancestor Spirit
Mam Waalatj	....	Eagle Hawk Man
Bami	....	Lost girl
Dwert	....	Bami's dog
Bami's Ngangk	....	Her mother
Bami's Maman	....	Her father
Mam Norn	....	Snake Man
Manga Djurang	....	Lizard Girl
Mam Maarang	....	Wind Man; *maar* is 'wind'
Wanbar	....	Whirlwind
Yok Yungung	....	Rain Woman; *yungu* is 'rain'
Djanak	....	Devil Spirit
Jidi Jidi	....	Willy Wagtail, a small black and white bird
Badja and Kaladari	....	The two sisters

The names of characters and other elements of this story are written in Nyungar, an Aboriginal language of southwest Australia. A pronunciation guide is on page 40.

A long time ago

A long time ago there lived a little girl called Bami. She was a beautiful child, full of fun and laughter. She had a pet dog, Dwert, who followed her everywhere.

Bami and her family lived among the Crow People, the Wardangmaat, in the southwest of Australia. They were nomadic people, and often walked great distances to hunt and gather food.

At night, when the stars came out and the moon shone overhead, the Burang and the Mandjang, the men and the women who were elders of the people, sat around the campfire and told the children wonderful stories about the dreamtime. Sometimes they talked about a magic place, where there were strange people and creatures.

Little Bami listened to these mysterious stories and felt strangely drawn back to that time.

So one day when the family was away hunting, Bami quietly left the camp and went walking in the bush, followed by Dwert. They had not got very far when a terrible whirlwind, a Wanbar, carried them away to the far away land. When the people discovered Bami missing they mourned her greatly.

Many years went by. Sometimes Bami's family talked about their lost little girl, but although the trackers searched, she had disappeared completely.

The Burang and the Mandjang shook their heads and whispered fearfully about the dreaded Djanak, and other mysterious creatures who lived in that far away place.

There were two little girls among the Wardangmaat who were sisters, named Badja and Kaladari. They were curious and asked Bami's family to tell them about the lost little girl, but Bami's parents were silent and sad because they had lost all hope of ever seeing their daughter again.

That night Badja had a dream. It was so real, like a vision, that she woke her sister and said, "Kaladari, I have had a dream about the lost little girl, Bami."

Her sister rubbed her eyes and said, "Tell me about it in the morning." But Badja begged her to stay awake and listen to her.

"My dream was about that far away place. The bush was all green and gold, with brightly coloured flowers, birds, reptiles and insects." She smiled.

"I saw a butterfly spirit sitting on a flower, and I remember it so clearly." She paused.

"Then I saw the clearing, of green grass, with strange people and animals sitting in a circle. In the middle of the circle was a big stone, and sitting on it was a girl and a dog, and a young man. He was handsome and brightly coloured, and behind him was the shadow of a beautiful snake. The young man was talking to the girl, and waving his arms, but she turned from him in fear." Tears came into Badja's eyes, and Kaladari tried to comfort her. "It was only a dream, Badja!"

But her sister did not answer. Then she said, "The girl saw me, and held out her arms, and cried, 'Take me away!' I tried to answer her but my voice would not come."

"Poor thing, Bami must be grown up now," Kaladari said, practically. "Oh, I know," Badja agreed. "She is much older than we are."

"Why don't you tell the Burang and the Mandjang about your dream?" said Kaladari. "They are so wise, and they could tell you what it means."

Badja nodded. She was very tired, and lay down on her fur-skin rug. Soon she and Kaladari were fast asleep.

The next day seemed to be very long for Badja. Would night ever come? But at last it was dark. The Mandjang and the Burang, those elder women and men, were sitting beside the campfire, and the children clustered around to hear their stories.

One of the Burang was telling them about the different clans of people; how Nurunderi, the great leader, taught them how to live in peace and harmony.

One of the Mandjang told them there were great stories about the dreaming, and that when they were older they would steadily learn more about these things.

Badja spoke fearfully to the whole gathering, "Please, can I talk? I have had a dream too."

They were surprised to hear little Badja speak.

The elders did not answer, and little Badja hurried on. "I know that you are all very wise. Will you tell me the meaning of a dream I had about the lost girl, Bami?"

Bami's mother, her Ngangk, answered, "Tell us about your dream, Badja."

The little girl told them about her frightening dream, and added, "I must try to find her, because she is afraid."

But Bami's mother looked very sad and shook her head. One of the Burang looked into the fire, then he answered, "You, Badja, and your sister Kaladari, have knowledge of the bush and you can live off the land. It will be enough."

Badja was disappointed. "But what is the meaning of my dream?"

He answered simply, "You must think about it. You, yourself, will know which way to go."

"What will I do?" cried Badja.

"Follow your dream," the Burang replied.

"What are we going to do, Badja?" whispered Kaladari.

"We must go tonight, or it will be too late," said Badja.

"What will we take?"

"Only our dilly bags, and a few skins. We can live on bush food, and we can find water. The bush creatures will help us too."

Kaladari was puzzled. "I can't understand why Bami is frightened. You said that the bush creatures were kind to her, and Dwert the dog is with her."

"Yes, the people and the creatures love her, but she is afraid because Mam Norn, the Snake Man, wants to marry her. Bami knows that she must return to her family. She already has a promised husband, Mam Waalatj, the Eagle Hawk Man, and there is much that she must learn before she goes to him."

At that moment a big cloud came over the moon, and it was dark.

"Come Kaladari, we must leave now."

The girls crept away from the camp and, although it was night, they were not afraid. The animals were their friends and would keep them safe.

Badja and Kaladari walked tirelessly all night, until at last the sun sent its golden rays over the bushland. The girls were enchanted with the beauty of the dawn.

The bush was fresh and beautiful. It was wonderful to hear the birds singing, and to see the exquisite butterfly spirits and brilliant flowers.

Little animals peeped at them curiously with bright eyes. At last they came to a place where there was water, clear as crystal, with pink and white lilies floating on the surface.

The girls had a swim in the pool. It was cool and refreshing. Then they gathered nuts and berries and dug up some bardi. It was hard work and they had to dig deep, but the grubs were delicious. After this they were very thirsty. They found the spring in the rocks, so they had cold water to drink.

The day was hot, but it was cool beside the pool. Badja decided that they would have to rest, for she did not know which way to go. She was afraid. Kaladari was not worried, because she believed that Badja would find a way.

Later in the day they made a fire. Then they both curled up in their skin rugs, and slept until next morning.

At dawn water spirits scrambled out of the pool and gazed curiously at the sleeping children, who were just waking up. How BIG they were! They tiptoed closer.

Badja opened her eyes and Kaladari sat up.

"Where are we?" they both cried.

One brave little water lily spirit flew over to Badja, and stood on her outstretched hand.

"You are beside our pool, and we are water lily spirits," she told them.

The girls were excited. Perhaps the spirits would help them.

"Can I tell you a story?" Badja asked.

"A story! A story! How wonderful!" they cried. So Badja told them the story of Bami, who had been taken away by Wanbar the whirlwind, so many years ago. Then she asked them for their help.

Sadly, they shook their heads. No, they couldn't help, but did Badja know about Jidi Jidi the wagtail?

"He is clever and cunning," they told her. "So why not ask him? Why not?"

He was actually quite close to them, sitting on the branch of a tree, but he just laughed.

"Why should I help you? You are from the Crow People! You know the secrets of the bush. So find out! Find out!"

Badja feared the Willy Wagtail, and knew that he was not to be trusted.

"But where shall we go? Which path shall we take? If only I was more clever!" poor Badja cried.

Then her eyes brightened. "I could ask Maar the wind and Yungu the rain. They go everywhere."

"But would they help us, Badja?" asked Kaladari.

Mam Maarang, the Wind Man, had been listening but he was invisible. Then they heard a great gust of laughter, with puffs in between. Mam Maarang became visible.

Badja and Kaladari saw a big shadowy form with great misty wings.

"So you want my help?" he puffed.

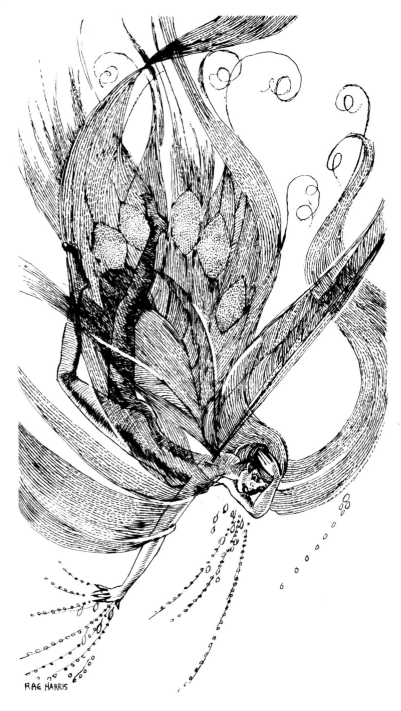

RAE HARRIS

The girls were frightened and ran away in fear.

Suddenly a lovely woman appeared, clad in silvery drapes and shimmering with rainbow colours.

"I am Yok Yungung, the Rain Woman," she explained. "Do not fear Mam Maarang, for we are here to help you."

"Why should I help?" growled Mam Maarang. "It was I who stole the child, and carried her away over the plains to the far away people. She is very happy!"

"You know she is not," the soft wailing rain cried. "She wants her Ngangk, her mother, and her family, and she is lonely."

"He is not really heartless," she went on, "but he is changeable."

"Oh, am I?" puffed Mam Maarang. "So are you, Yok Yungung. You can be terrible."

Badja was impatient. Time was going by.

"Jidi Jidi, the wagtail, knows where the far away people are," Yungu said.

Badja saw the Willy Wagtail watching them.

"Jidi Jidi," she cried, hopefully. "You are so clever, no one is as cunning or as wonderful as you are. Please help us with a little of your wisdom."

Jidi Jidi hopped about, fluttering his tail, his little white breast nearly bursting with pride.

"Why should I? I am too busy a fellow to find your lost child," he said, importantly, "and anyway, I do not wish to help you! Why don't you go to the Wise Woman, Yok Dwongkabula?"

"Yok Dwongkabula?" The girls stared at him in surprise. "Where is she? Where can we find her?"

But Jidi Jidi only laughed, and flew away.

Badja cried. "I remember the elders telling us about the Wise One, Yok Dwongkabula, how she lived a long time within the stillness of the earth until Mamang, the Great Spirit, called her to awaken the grass, plants and trees.

RAE HARRIS

"She made her home on the great sandy plain, and then set out on a journey, from north to south, then east to west. As she walked, grass and plants sprang up in her footprints. Now she helps people and creatures with her wisdom."

Kaladari was excited. "Do you think we will find her, Badja?"

Badja turned to the wind and rain. "Oh, what can we do?" she cried, tearfully.

At last Mam Maarang took pity on them.

"We will summon the spirits of the wind and the rain. They can cover great distances and spaces. On their return they will tell you which way to go."

He called the wind spirits with a terrific sound of rushing air, but the girls were no longer afraid of him. Then Yok Yungung called for the spirits of the rain, and suddenly the air was filled with the sound of the wings of the spirits of the wind and rain.

"What is your wish?" asked their leader.

RAE HARRIS

Mam Maarang told them to find the Wise Woman, Yok Dwongkabula, and to return swiftly. The spirits vanished in a whirlwind, and the girls prepared for the journey with new hope. In almost no time the spirits returned.

"We have found the Wise Woman's camp," the leader told Mam Maarang. Badja and Kaladari were on their way at last. They climbed on to the back of the wind, between the huge wings of Mam Maarang, and were borne into the sky, with Yok Yungung following.

The girls were excited, their hearts were beating fast. "I am sure we will find Bami now," cried Kaladari. They looked down at the tree tops. The pool had vanished from view. Soon they found themselves coming back to earth, landing in a rainbow of colour.

The Wise Woman's camp was a mass of tiny everlasting flowers. Then they saw Yok Dwongkabula herself, as beautiful as the elders had described. Grouped around her there were birds and animals, and among them was the Lizard Girl, Manga Djurang.

Badja and Kaladari stepped forward eagerly and took Yok Dwongkabula's hands in welcome. Maar the wind, and Yungu the rain had become invisible again.

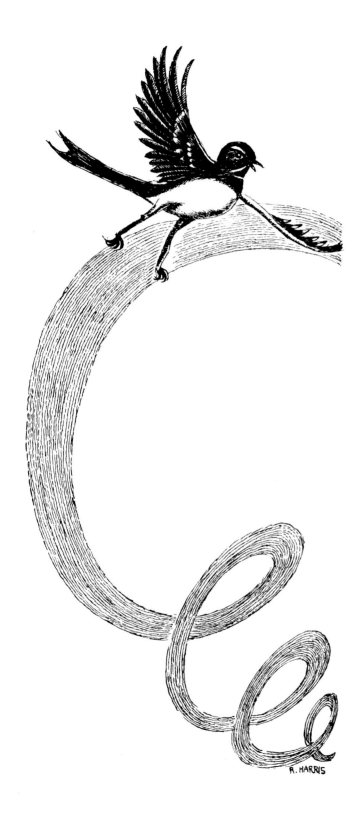

"I welcome you, Badja and Kaladari. You have come a long way to find me."

"Wise Woman, we have come a long way because of a dream I had about a lost girl of the Wardangmaat."

"And you have come to me for help?" asked Yok Dwongkabula. Badja nodded. "Jidi Jidi told us of your great wisdom and kindness."

But the Willy Wagtail was sorry that he had helped them. Badja had flattered him into telling her about the Wise Woman. At that moment he was flying away to warn the far away people. "The girl, Bami, is in great danger. You must hurry if you are to save her," said Yok Dwongkabula. Then she warned, "But you cannot release Bami unless someone else takes her place on the stone."

"Who can take Bami's place?" cried the girls.

"The true wife for the Snake Man is Manga Djurang, the Lizard Girl," Yok Dwongkabula told them. "You must steal Bami, and leave Manga Djurang on the stone," the Wise Woman explained. "She is the rightful wife for the Snake Man and must take her place beside him. They will understand each other and she can be his wife."

The Lizard Girl turned to Yok Dwongkabula in surprise. "Has the time come for me to join my husband, Wise Woman?"

"Yes," Yok Dwongkabula answered. "Mam Norn, the Snake Man, is waiting for you." The lovely Lizard Girl came forward, smiling. "I am happy that the time has come."

Yok Dwongkabula said goodbye to Manga Djurang, and then she warned the children to waste no time. "The wagtail won't," she said. "You must get there before he does. Mam Maarang and Yok Yungung will take you there."

The wind and the rain became visible, so the girls and Manga Djurang climbed between the great wings of Mam Maarang. Yok Yungung flew beside them, and they were carried away over the tree tops.

Soon they were descending back to earth, and they landed softly on the ground, just beyond the clearing. "Look!" cried Badja. "It's exactly what I saw in my dream!"

There was a circle of people and animals. Bami's dog was standing beside her, and Mam Norn, the Snake Man, was talking to her. Bami's eyes were wide with fear. Mam Norn was very handsome and his golden brown skin shimmered with many colours.

RAE HARRIS

Then Mam Maarang told them what he must do. "I am going to destroy the meeting, as Wanbar the whirlwind. The people will be blown away. Then we must take Bami and Dwert quickly, and Manga Djurang must take her place on the stone." He became Wanbar the whirlwind. Roaring and shrieking, Wanbar whirled into the centre of the clearing. Then Yok Yungung cried and cried, and the rain came down in torrents.

The Snake Man tried to grasp Bami, but Wanbar swept her and the howling Dwert away from him. Manga Djurang, the Lizard Girl, ran forward and sat on the stone beside the astonished Snake Man. He gazed at the beautiful young creature and smiled.

Jidi Jidi arrived too late to warn anyone. He was swept away by Wanbar, and soaked with rain by Yok Yungung. They had decided that he needed a lesson! He wasn't so clever after all. His feathers were nearly blown off. He was cold and shivery, and very sorry for himself. Wanbar and Yok Yungung continued to shriek and cry until the girls were safely out of the way.

When the reptiles, birds and animals returned, they were broken hearted to see that Bami had at last escaped. Then they saw the lovely Lizard Girl, Manga Djurang. She was sitting on the stone, gazing happily at Mam Norn the Snake Man, who was holding her hands in his. They spoke gently to each other.

The far away people rejoiced that the Wise Woman had sent them the Lizard Girl, a fitting wife for their beloved Snake Man. Now they would all be happy for ever.

Safe in the bush, Bami turned to the girls. "Oh, Badja and Kaladari, take me back to my people!" Mam Maarang's great wings became visible once more, and the girls told Bami and Dwert how wonderful it was to ride on his huge back.

The gentle rain smiled. "I will fly beside Mam Maarang," she said, "and you will be safe."

How marvellous it was to ride over the tree tops!

At last, in the distance, they saw smoke curling into the sky, and then the camp of their own Crow People, the Wardangmaat! The sun had gone down, and it was almost night - story time - when the children join the family circle round the campfire and are taught by their Mandjang and Burang.

Suddenly there was a terrific whirring sound. The people ran out of the Mayas, their shelters, and all stared into the sky. Mam Maarang and Yok Yungung alighted gently at the edge of the clearing.

Badja, Kaladari, Bami and Dwert slid off the huge back of Mam Maarang, and the children turned to say goodbye to the spirits of the wind and the rain. But Mam Maarang and Yok Yungung had disappeared. All they heard was the rustle of the gentle breeze and the sound of raindrops falling gently on to the earth. The people ran forward and caught the children in their arms.

Bami's Ngangk and Maman folded their long lost daughter to their hearts. Everyone cried and cried for her, and then the whole family welcomed them back. Bami's faithful dog Dwert was hugged and loved by the children.

Mam Waalatj, the young Eagle Hawk Man, came forward and took Bami's hand. They smiled at each other, and were happy. As for Badja and Kaladari, they rejoiced.

"My dream has come true!" said Badja.

The bush scented night was now still. The Burang and the Mandjang sat by the crackling fire with the children. They only smiled.

Nyungar Alphabet and Pronunciation

The spelling system used in this book for Nyungar words includes the following symbols:

p	t	rt	tj	k
b	d	rd	dj	
m	n	rn	ny	ng
	l	rl	ly	
		r	rr	
w			y	
a	e	i	o	u

The sounds written as *rt*, *rd*, *rn* and *rl* are pronounced with the tip of the tongue drawn well back and placed against the palate.

Sounds written as *tj*, *dj*, *ny* and *ly* are pronounced with the top of the tongue resting against the palate.

The *ng* sound, which often occurs at the beginning of words, is pronounced just like the 'ng' in *singer* (not as in *finger*, which would be written 'fingka').

The double R-sound, *rr* is sometimes pronounced as a trill, sometimes as a fast tap of the tongue against the roof of the mouth, as in *butter*.

The vowel *a* is usually pronounced like the short vowel sound in *cut*. The longer vowel written as *aa* is pronounced like the 'a' in *father*.

The *u* vowel is never pronounced like the 'u' in English *cut*, but like the 'u' vowel in *put*, or the 'oo' in *foot*.

All other sounds have much the same value as they do in English.

About Diney

Dinah was born at Wedge Station near Port Hedland on Christmas Day, as she said, 'a long time ago'. She had not been told in what year. Her mother was a young Aboriginal woman employed at the station homestead, and her father the station owner.

She told me that her childhood was happy, with many friends at the station. Dinah spoke sadly about a horse, Black Diamond, she had to leave when she came south to Perth, more than a thousand kilometres away.

My mother brought her to see me at a time when I had a small son, eighteen months, and another child almost ready to make its appearance. I was also trying to keep up my painting. From that day, Dinah became a member of our household, although sometimes she would leave for a month or two or as long as a year. Dinah often told the children stories that she had been told as a girl and their favourite was about a Willy Wagtail, who was very naughty!

One day Dinah departed, and then a few years later she somehow heard the news of another addition to our family, and rang me up. "You can't have a baby without me," she said. "I am coming back."

Dinah was a part of our life as a family for about twenty years and it is she who inspired this book.

Rae Harris

About the Dream

When Rae told me she was writing a story that came from the dreamtime, I told her about the differences between people in the north and the south. The languages and many things of importance are different. The story would affect many Aboriginal people in many places, so I felt I should advise her on our history and culture. Then she showed me her drawings and I thought they were beautiful. We had the same sort of feeling about painting, even though I do designs where she paints a face.

So I spent a lot of time talking with Rae and Cliff about our culture and languages. She would say something, and I would say, "What do you mean?" so she would explain, but I'd be different, and Cliff would say to Rae, "That's her way, you've got to listen." I have known them for some years and become very close to them. We are now working on another book.

Beryl Harp

Rae Harris, HRMS, was born in Geraldton, Western Australia, in 1905. Her mother was born in Farina, a small railway siding on the Ghan Line near Oodnadatta. Stories from Aboriginal people who lived there were retold to Rae during her own childhood. Rae settled in Perth, marrying Cliff Harris in 1936. She is an Honorary member of the Royal Miniature Society and has contributed to two books on the techniques of painting.

Beryl Harp was born at Brookton, Western Australia, in 1936. She is a gifted contemporary Aboriginal painter, whose work is also used in fabric and clothing design. Beryl is a community worker with an interest in the preservation of her culture and is helping to re-establish an area of bushland called Kulbardi (Magpie) in suburban Perth, not far from where she lives with husband Leo Harp and their four children.

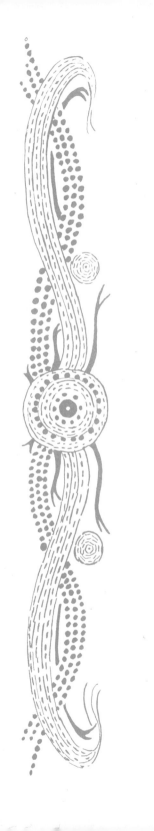